JALLIANWALA BAGH: A REVOLUTIONARY HISTORY OF THE 1919 MASSACRE

GOLU KUMAR

Contents

1. Chapter 1   1

1

This chapter will provide a brief account of what happened in Punjab during the turbulent years of 1919. Knowing about these episodes, also referred to as "the Punjab wrongs," is crucial to understanding what has transpired in India subsequently and how they affected the relationship between England and India. We'll start with the start of World War I and move on to key episodes in the order they happened.

It is a matter of common knowledge now that the people of India supported the British Empire throughout the war in a very liberal and enthusiastic manner. "India's contributions to the war both in its quota of man-force and money were far beyond the capacity of its poor inhabitants." Leaders of all states of the opinion joined hands to assist the Empire in its time of need. It has been stated before that Gandhi was overworked in their capacity as an honorary recruiting officer until he contracted dysentery, which at one time threatened to prove fatal.

India was "bled white" to win the war. But for her support of men and money England would have suffered greatly in prestige. Except for Indian troops the German advance to Paris in the fall of 1914 might not have been checked. The official publication, "India's Contribution to the Great War," describes the work of the Indian troops thus:

"The Indian Corps reached France in the nick of time and helped
to stem the great German thrust towards Ypres and the Channel
Ports during the Autumn of 1914. These were the only trained
reinforcements immediately available in any part of the British
Empire and right worthily they played their part.

"In Egypt and Palestine, in Mesopotamia, Persia, East, and West
Africa and in subsidiary theaters, they shared with their British
and Dominion comrades the attainment of final victory."

While the issue of the war still seemed doubtful, the British Parliament, to induce the people of India to still greater efforts in their support of the Empire, held out definite promises of self-government to India after the war as a reward for their loyalty. Mr. Montague, His Majesty's Secretary of State for India, made the following announcement on August 20, 1917:

"The policy of His Majesty's Government with which the Government
of India are in complete accord, is that of the increasing
association of Indians in every branch of the administration and
the gradual development of self-governing institutions with a view
to the progressive realization of responsible government in India
as an integral part of the British Empire. They have decided that

substantial steps in this direction should be taken as soon as

possible, ..."

The text of the above announcement was widely published in the entire press of India. Then followed the famous message of President Woodrow Wilson to Congress with its definite pledge of "self-determination" to subordinate nations. This helped to brighten still more India's hopes for home rule.

Naturally, after the Armistice was signed, the people of India expected the fulfillment of the war promises. "But the British Government, anticipating that soon after the war ended there would be a loud clamor in the country for home-rule, gave instead of self-government the Rowlatt Act, which was designed to stifle the nationalistic spirit in its infancy." The act gave unlimited power to the police to prohibit public assemblies, to order indiscriminate searches of private homes, to make arrests without notification, and so forth. "Its main purpose was in such a manner to strengthen the authority of the police and to enable them to root out of the country every form of liberal and independent thought." The plans of the British Bureaucracy were, however, defeated in their entirety, because the passage of the act did not go through the Legislative Assembly as smoothly as was expected. The whole country cried out in one voice against the Rowlatt Act, but it was passed by the British Government of India in the teeth of the _unanimous_ opposition of _all_ elected as well as government-appointed Indian members of the Legislative Council.

This was once again followed by mass meetings and parades in protest, petitions to the British Parliament, delegations to the Viceroy, and a nationwide demonstration against the Rowlatt Act. But the Government altogether ignored the sentiments of the country in this matter, an attitude which in turn helped to inflame the masses still more.

Gandhi considered the existence of the act on the statute books of India a national humiliation, and in protest, he ordered the people of India to observe April 6, 1919, as a day of fast and national _hartal_. _Hartal_ is the sign of deep mourning, during which the whole business of the country is stopped and the people wonder about the streets in grief and lamentation. It was observed in ancient times only at the death of popular kings or on the occasion of some other very serious national calamity.

The response to Gandhi's appeal for the _hartal_ was very general. It was surprising how quickly the sentiment of national consciousness had spread throughout the country. Overnight Gandhi's name was on the lips of everybody, and even the most ignorant countrywomen were talking about the Rowlatt Act. I remember that on the afternoon of April the 6th, while I was walking toward the site of the mass meeting in my town, the like of which were being held all over India, and at which resolutions of protest against the Rowlatt Act were passed, I saw a girl of six nearly collapse on the street. After I had picked her up, and she had rested from the heat of the sun, I asked her who she was and where she was going. The little girl replied: "I am the daughter of _Bharat Mata_ (Mother India) and I am going to the funeral of Daulat (Rowlatt). Mahatma Gandhi (Gandhi) has called me."

The day passed quite peacefully except for slight disturbances in a few places. But the excitement throughout the country, particularly in Punjab, was very great. The situation was so tense that Gandhi sent his strong admonitions of non-violence to his people in a continual stream. The activity at Amritsar started when, on the morning of April 10th the English Commissioner invited Dr. Kitchlew and Dr. Satyapal, the two popular young leaders of the city, to his residence and ordered their deportation to some unknown place. When it became known that their leaders had been treacherously removed the citizens went on a sudden _hartal_, and a huge mob began to gather in front of the main city gate. The mob soon organized itself into a procession, which started to move toward the District Commissioner's residence to request the restoration of Doctors Kitchlew and Satyapal. While crossing the railroad bridge, the procession was met by armed police who soon caused six casualties among the peaceful, unarmed mob. The mob soon turned back and fell upon the city in a wild fury. It divided itself into different groups and expended its rage by setting fire to the city hall, two English banks, and a local Christian church. Two bank managers, the only Englishmen present in town on that day, were cruelly murdered. An English nurse who happened to be passing through a narrow street was also assaulted by the mob, but was soon rescued by the citizens and carried to a place of safety. Later on, this benevolent Christian lady greatly endeared herself to the people of Amritsar by refusing to accept any other indemnity for the assault than the price of her wrist watch which was lost in the scramble.

Immediately after the news of Amritsar reached the other towns in the province, similar outbreaks of popular frenzy occurred in many places, with this difference, however, that at no other place besides Amritsar were English residents injured. There were casualties on the side of the mob everywhere, but none on the side of the English. On April 11th the authority of the civil government was withdrawn, and martial law was declared in most sections of the province of Punjab.

Thus did the trouble begin that resulted in the massacre of Amritsar. On that fatal day, April 13th, a mass meeting had been announced to take place in Jallianwalla Bagh, an open enclosure in the heart of the city of Amritsar. As it happened, April 13th was also Baisakhi day, which is observed all over India as a day of a national festival. Large crowds of country people had gathered in the city on that account. On the morning of the 13th, General Dyer, the commanding officer of the city, issued from the headquarters an order prohibiting the Jallianwalla Bagh meeting, and notices to that effect were posted in several places in the city. It should be mentioned here that unlike the towns of America, there were in Amritsar at the time no universally read daily papers which could convey the Commanding Officer's order all around in the short interval between its issue and the time of the meeting. Under these circumstances, General Dyer's prohibitory order could reach only a small fraction of the people in the city.

Now let us come to the scene of the meeting. People began to assemble in Jallianwalla Bagh at 3 o'clock. There were old men, women who carried babies in their arms, and children who held toys in their hands. They were all dressed in their holiday gala dresses. "While a few had come there to attend the meeting knowingly, the majority had just followed the crowd and drifted in the Bagh out of simple curiosity." Whatever may have been its nature otherwise, certainly, the crowd at the Jallianwalla was not composed of bloody revolutionists. Not one of them carried even a walking stick. They had assembled there in the open enclosure peacefully to listen to speeches and perhaps at the end to pass a few resolutions. At four o'clock the meeting was called to order, and the speeches began. No more than forty minutes after this peaceful gathering, the audience was listening in an attentive and orderly manner to the speaker who stood on a raised platform in the center when General Dyer walked in with his band of thirty soldiers and suddenly opened fire on the crowd without giving them any warning or chance to disperse. There was a sudden wild skirmish in the enclosure. People began to run toward all sides to save their lives; those who fell were run over by the rest and crushed under their weight. Others who attempted to escape by leaping over the low wall on the east end were shot dead by the fire from the general's squad. As the crowd centered near the only escape from the unfinished low wall, the general directed his shots there. He aimed where the crowd was the thickest, and inside of the fifteen minutes during which his ammunition lasted he had killed at least eight hundred men, women, and children and wounded many times that number.

It was already late afternoon when General Dyer, his ammunition had run out, departed to his headquarters without providing any kind of succor or medical aid to the wounded who lay bleeding and helpless at the scene of slaughter. Before the people of the neighborhood recovered from their consternation, it had already begun to get dark. As one of the rules of martial law strictly forbade walking in the streets of Amritsar after dark, no person or group of persons could bring organized relief to the wounded at Jallianwalla. The horrible agonies of those that lay in the Bagh disabled and deserted were heard with grim patience all through the night by the faithful wife Rattan Devi when she sat there "amid that ghastly human carnival" holding in her lap the dead body of her beloved husband. She had run to the scene after the shooting in a mad search for her husband. After she had looked underneath a dozen heaps of dead bodies and stumbled over many others, her eyes were drawn to the spot where her husband's dead body lay flat on the ground. Rattan Devi's husband was already dead and beyond human aid. The devoted wife could not restore the dead man to life, but how could she afford to leave his lifeless body in the stark neighborhood overnight? She was too weak to carry it home all by herself and there was no aid available. So she sat there through the night holding a dead man in her lap.

The horrors of that night of suffering were related by Rattan Devi in her evidence before the Indian National Congress sub-committee, in which she described "the fearful agony of dying human beings, who kept crying for drinks of water all through the night." No friendly aid came to these departing souls in their last hours of deep distress. Afraid of General Dyer's deadly vengeance their fellowmen had stayed away, while dogs from the neighboring streets wandered freely inside the Bagh to feast on the bleeding human bodies.

At the following session of the Indian National Congress which was held at Amritsar, I saw at its exhibition twenty pairs of little shoes, belonging to babies from a few months to a year old. These had been picked up in the Jallianwalla Bagh by various persons after the shooting, and they belonged to twenty innocent babies in their mothers' laps who had been completely obliterated in the mad scramble that had accompanied the shooting. All that was left of these children were those tiny shoes. May God bless the souls of the dear little ones and many others who fell victims to the haughty general's bloody mood on the thirteenth of April, 1919, at Jallianwalla Bagh.

Later, when General Dyer was cross-examined before Lord Hunter's Committee, which was appointed by the British Parliament to report on Punjab disturbances, he testified to the following:

1. That there was no provocation on the part of the people of Amritsar for the Jallianwalla Bagh massacre either on the day of the shooting or immediately before it. He had the situation well in hand and the atmosphere was quite calm and peaceful.

2. That his order prohibiting the meeting was issued the morning before the meeting and reached only a fraction of the people in Amritsar on that festival day of the thirteenth.

3. That when he arrived on the scene of the meeting with his squad, he found the people calmly listening to the speaker and there was no show of resistance offered to him. On the other hand, on seeing him enter the premises, the audience began to run off in all directions.

4. That he opened fire at the assembled meeting without giving the people any warning or chance to disperse, and he continued firing while his ammunition lasted--all the time directing his shots at places where the crowd was the thickest.

5. That the path was too tiny for him to fit his machine gun inside, so he had to leave it outside. And he acknowledged that if he had been able to use the machine gun, the number of victims would have been far higher.

6. That he carried out the carnage at the Jallianwalla to instill a lesson in the populace, and that he continued to fire after the audience started to disperse because of fear that they would mock him. The general wished to demonstrate to the populace the power of British rule.

7. He failed to consider or care about helping the injured in Jallianwalla. It wasn't related to his line of work.

A portion of General Dyer's testimony before Lord Hunter's committee is reproduced below:

"Q. What did you do when you entered the Bagh? A. I started firing.

How soon? A. Right away. I believe it didn't take me more than thirty seconds to decide what my job was after giving the situation some thought.

How big was the crowd, exactly? A. I then put their number at around 5,000. I later learned that there were a lot more.

Q. On the assumption that there was that risk of people being in the crowd who were not aware of the proclamation, did it not occur to you that it was a proper measure to ask the crowd to disperse before you took that step of actually firing? A. No, at the time I did not. I merely felt that my orders had not been obeyed, that martial law was flouted, and that it was my duty to immediately disperse by rifle fire.

Q. When you left Rambagh [his headquarters] did it occur to you that you might have to fire? A. Yes, I had considered the nature of the duty that I might have to face.

Q. Did the crowd at once start to disperse as soon as you fired? A. Immediately.

Q. Did you continue firing? A. Yes.

Q. What reason had you to suppose that if you had ordered the assembly to leave the Bagh, they would not have done so without the necessity of your firing and continuing firing for any length of time? A. Yes, I think it quite possible that I could have dispersed them perhaps even without firing.

Q. Why did you not have recourse to that? A. They would have all comeback and laughed at me, and I should have made what I considered a fool of myself.

Q. And on counting the ammunition it was found that 1,650 rounds of ammunition had been fired? A. Quite right.

Q. Supposing the passage was sufficient to allow the armored cars to go in, would you have opened fire with the machine guns? A. I think, probably, yes.

Q. In that case the casualties would have been very much higher?

A. Yes. Q. I take it that your idea in taking that action was to strike terror? A. Call it what you like. I was going to punish them. My idea from the military point of view was to make a wide impression."

During its history mankind has witnessed many massacres of a bloody and ruthless nature, but in every case, before a massacre occurred, there was a provocation of some kind. Jallianwalla Bagh stands out unique in this respect--that it was an unprovoked, premeditated and pre-arranged, coldblooded massacre of at least eight hundred innocent men, women, and children, who were assembled in a peaceful meeting on the day of their national festival, with no thought of evil in their minds nor any desire to offer resistance of any sort or kind to anybody.

The most interesting part of the story is that what had happened at Jallianwalla Bagh on the thirteenth of April was considered so trivial and unimportant a matter that it took four months for the news to reach official London. After the report of Lord Hunter's committee had been published, and all the horrible details of the massacre were fully disclosed, General Dyer was retired from the military service on full pension. But on his return to England, he was handed a purse of ten thousand pounds sterling, which amount had been raised by voluntary subscription by the English people to recompense the general for his heroic work at Jallianwalla Bagh. Such was the reaction of the

English nation to the massacre.

Gandhi's interpretation of General Dyer's "heroism" is, however, different. He writes:

"He [General Dyer] has called an unarmed crowd of men and

children--mostly holiday-makers--'a rebel army.' He believes himself to be the savior of Punjab in that he was able to

shoot down like rabbits men who were penned in an enclosure.

Such a man is unworthy of being considered a soldier. there was

no bravery in his action. He ran no risk. He shot without the slightest opposition and without warning. This is not an 'error of

judgment'. It is a paralysis of it in the face of fancied danger. It is proof of criminal incapacity and heartlessness."

The reader will be in a position now to understand the meaning of Mahatma Gandhi's letter to the Viceroy of India, dated August 1, 1920, and quoted on page 114 in which Gandhi gave his reasons for his decision not to cooperate with the British Government of India. It may be recalled that one of Mahatma Gandhi's reasons was the "callous disregard of the feelings of Indians" betrayed by the House of Lords. It must be remembered here also that the massacre of Jallianwalla occurred on April 13, 1919, and it was exactly a year and three months later that Mahatma Gandhi made his decision to boycott the British Government. During this interval, he had persistently hoped for a change in the British attitude.

The massacre at Jallianwalla was only one part of the awful Punjab story. What occurred at Amritsar and other towns in the province during the martial days of 1919 was even more shameful and unworthy, "on account of the outrage of human dignity is involved." The issuing of crawling orders and the throwing of bombs from airplanes over peaceful towns constituted in part the doings of the military and police during the unfortunate days of martial law. Nor was that all. Mrs. Sarojini Naidu, the first woman president of India, said while speaking on the "Punjab wrongs" before a large London audience (Kingsway Hall, June 3, 1919):

My sisters were flogged, they were stripped naked; they were

outraged."

The ingenuity of the English officials during the martial law period in inventing fancy punishments showed itself conspicuously in the town of Kasur where according to the findings of the Congress sub-committee,

"1. There was no mention of any violation of the martial law; instead, schoolboys and men were spanked "without any particular object." They invited prostitutes to attend the ceremony.

2. People were made to climb ladders and keep time.

3. Lime was used to cleanse religious wanderers.

4. People were made to rub their roses on the ground if they didn't salute Europeans.

6. Public gallows were built but later taken down. During the martial law era, 18 people were hung in Punjab, and many of them were completely innocent.

The testimony Gurdevi, the widow of Mangal Jat, provided to the congressional subcommittee regarding what had happened in Manianwalla is provided below:

"One day, during the Martial Law period, Mr. Bosworth Smith

gathered together all the males of over eight years at the

Dacca Dalia Bungalow, which is some miles from our

village, in

connection with the investigations that were going on. Whilst the

men were at the Bungalow, he rode to our village, taking back with

him all the women who met him on the way carrying food for their

men at the Bungalow. Reaching the village, he went around the

lanes and ordered all women to come out of their houses, himself

forcing them out with sticks. He made us all stand near the village Daira. The women folded their hands before him. He beat

some with his stick and spat at them and used the foulest and most

unmentionable language. He hit me twice and spat in my face...

"He repeatedly called us she-asses, bitches, flies, and swine and

said: 'You were in the same beds with your husbands; why did you

not prevent them from going out to do mischief? Now your skirts

will be looked at by the Police Constables'. He kicked me also

and ordered us to undergo the torture of holding our ears bypass

our arms around the legs, whilst being bent double.

"This treatment was met out to us in the absence of our men who

were at the Bungalow."

Cowardice, thy name is Bosworth Smith! Moral degradation in a human being could not go any lower than this. Search the entire history of mankind, and you will fail to find the equal of this act in its ferocity and barbarism. How curious! The world believes still that England's mission in India is that of civilizing backward people.

The Jallianwalla massacre and other "Punjab wrongs" gave a great impetus to the nationalist movement in India. What the Indian National Congress had failed to accomplish in its steady work of thirty-two years, the Punjab persecutions and humiliations did in the course of a few months. It has helped to arouse in the minds of the people of India a powerful national consciousness. It has been truly said that the blood of the martyrs at Jallianwalla Bagh has made the heart of all of India bleed.

Those who ask the question, "Why does India revolt?" may find a part of their answer in the word "Jallianwalla Bagh."

Quoted from Lajpat Rai's _Unhappy India_.

www.ingramcontent.com/pod-product-compliance
Lightning Source LLC
Chambersburg PA
CBHW030237150726
47988CB00020B/1711